# I AM PRINCESS

Tyneisha Collins

# ACKNOWLEDGEMENT

I would like to thank the only father I've ever known, My Father GOD, the KING of all KINGS for blessing me with gifts that will inspire children all over the world. Without you, none of my accomplishments would have been possible! My whole entire existence is a product of your unconditional love and mercy for me!

Tyneisha Renai Collins

*Dedicated to all the PRINCESSES in the whole entire world, you all matter!*

P is for the PRETTY face that I see looking back at me, each and every time I look at myself in the Mirror.

I AM PRINCESS!

R is for my ROYAL inheritance which was passed down to me from the King Of All Kings, My Father GOD.

I AM PRINCESS!

I is for the IMAGINATION I have that
allows me to dream really BIG about
what I want to be when I grow up.

I AM PRINCESS!

N is for my NATURAL ability to Love everyone Unconditionally no matter what their imperfections are.

I AM PRINCESS!

C is for my CONFIDENCE which reminds me that I CAN conquer the world with my GOD giving gifts.

I AM PRINCESS!

E is for Enough, I am more than enough, so valued that GOD sacrificed his only son for my life.

I AM PRINCESS!

S is for my STRENGTH, I know that I Can Do All Things Through CHRIST, Who Strengthens Me.

I AM PRINCESS!

S is a reminder of just how SPECIAL I am to all the people in my life that Love and Adore ME.

I AM PRINCESS!

Because of all these many things, I AM PRINCESS and as I continue to grow older and learn more, I will blossom into a Beautiful and Magnificent QUEEN!

# NOTES

## (What Makes You A Princess)

_____

_____

_____

_____

_____

_____

_____

_____

Made in the USA
Middletown, DE
17 January 2021